P9-DIW-739

HOOP DANCER DETERMINATION

BY JAKE MADDOX

Text by Stacy Wells

Illustrated by Jesus Aburto

STONE ARCH BOOKS

a capstone imprint

Published by Stone Arch Books, an imprint of Capstone
1710 Roe Crest Drive, North Mankato, Minnesota 56003
capstonepub.com

Library of Congress Cataloging-in-Publication Data
Names: Maddox, Jake, author. | Wells, Stacy, author. | Aburto, Jesus, illustrator. | Maddox, Jake. Impact books. Jake Maddox sports story.
Title: Hoop dancer determination / Jake Maddox; text by Stacy Wells; illustrated by Jesus Aburto.
Description: North Mankato, Minnesota : Stone Arch Books, an imprint of Capstone, 2023. | Series: Jake Maddox sports stories | Audience: Ages 8–11. | Audience: Grades 4–6. | Summary: For the past two years, since attending a Choctaw Nation powwow with his family, thirteen-year-old Tobias has secretly been teaching himself how to hoop dance, but once his secret gets out, he must decide if he wants to share his dancing at the spring talent show.
Identifiers: LCCN 2022000805 (print) | LCCN 2022000806 (ebook) | ISBN 9781666344936 (hardcover) | ISBN 9781666353433 (paperback) | ISBN 9781666344974 (pdf)
Subjects: LCSH: Hoop dance—Juvenile fiction. | Hoop dancers—Juvenile fiction. | Choctaw boys—Juvenile fiction. | Self-confidence—Juvenile fiction. | Talent shows—Juvenile fiction. | Friendship—Juvenile fiction. | CYAC: Hoop dance—Fiction. | Choctaw Indians—Fiction. | Indians of North America—Fiction. | Self-confidence—Fiction. | Talent shows—Fiction. | Friendship—Fiction. | LCGFT: Fiction.
Classification: LCC PZ7.M25643 Hkv 2022 (print) | LCC PZ7.M25643 (ebook) | DDC 813.6 [Fic]--dc23/eng/20220124
LC record available at https://lccn.loc.gov/2022000805
LC ebook record available at https://lccn.loc.gov/2022000806

Designer: Heidi Thompson

Printed and bound in the USA. PO4882

TABLE OF CONTENTS

CHAPTER 1

ROLLING HOOPS

Thirteen-year-old Tobias Wilson's alarm clock beeped. The early morning sun played peekaboo through the single window in his room. He groaned, rubbed the sleep from his eyes, and stood.

"Time to get to work," he said. "The hoops are calling."

Tobias threw on basketball shorts, an old T-shirt, and shoes. He ran his hand through his dark hair. Then he tied a purple bandana around his head.

His mom and sisters were still asleep, so he tiptoed through the house. He grabbed his equipment bag and went out the back door.

The chill in the air pricked his skin. But he knew he'd warm up fast once he started dancing. This was Tobias's favorite time of the day. Just him and his hoops.

He turned on his music, keeping the volume low to not disturb the neighbors. Then he laid two hoops on the ground, keeping the third in his hand. An electronic powwow song from a popular Native band from Oklahoma gave a steady beat.

Tobias warmed up with a quick, one hoop side-arm circle on the left, then switched the hoop to the right. He then threw the hoop up in the air, spun on one foot, and caught the hoop with his left hand.

He repeated the pattern—left-right-throw-spin-catch, left-right-throw-spin-catch—until he was breathing heavy.

Tobias had picked up hoop dancing after attending an intertribal powwow with his family two years ago up in Oklahoma.

He'd always been a good dancer, but hoop dancing wasn't as easy as it looked. Especially if you were teaching yourself through videos online. There also weren't many Choctaw Nation hoop dancers. Tobias was one of only a few.

Again, he repeated the pattern, but after the spin he added a ground hoop roll. When it came back to him, he did the routine again.

Batting cages and golf ranges dotted his small Texas town, but there wasn't a hoop dancing store where he could ask for help. The only hoop dancer he knew lived over a hundred miles from Tobias's home. The dancer wasn't available to help with lessons or pointers.

His mom once danced ballet, but she quit when she was eighteen. Still, she gave him some basics. She said they'd help with his coordination and flexibility. And they did.

Tobias moved closer to the hoop on the ground. Twirling one hoop around with his left hand, his right foot stepped on the hoop. The hoop popped straight into his hand.

From there, he did figure eights with the hoops and spun. He threw up one and caught it, then did the same with the other. He repeated this move again because practice makes perfect. He was throwing a hoop in the air when—

"Hey, Tobias." Declan Harris popped his head over their shared fence. "What are you doing?"

Tobias froze. The hoops fell and rolled a few feet from him.

No one outside of family had ever seen him hoop dance. Not even Declan, his friend since kindergarten. Besides his nosy nature, he was a good friend.

"Are you playing with your sister's Hula-Hoops?" Declan asked. He leaned over the fence to get a better look. Without waiting for an answer, he added, "And I really like that music. It has a nice beat."

Tobias spun to turn down the music but tripped over the hoops instead. He fell face-first into his mom's herb patch, nose-to-leaf with the catnip.

CHAPTER 2

HOOP DANCING 101

"When did you start playing music early in the morning?" Declan asked as he entered Tobias's backyard. "Also, why are you sweating?"

"Declan, you ask a lot of questions," Tobias responded. He hurried to turn off the music.

Declan shrugged his shoulders. "That's what my mom says. And my teachers. The list goes on. But you didn't answer my questions."

Tobias bent down and picked up his hoops. He wasn't ready to tell Declan about his dancing. Nobody outside his family knew about his hoop dancing. "Guess I should go in and get ready for school," he said.

"Hold on a minute," Declan said. "Can I see one of your hoops? They're so cool and colorful."

Tobias held on to the hoop and thought. Should he tell Declan? If he didn't, Declan would never give up trying to find out. Tobias gave in.

Tobias handed over a hoop.

"It's a hoop used in hoop dancing," he said. "Traditionally, they are made from willow branches. But mine are made from plastic tubing. I use colored tape to decorate them."

"You made these?" Declan ran the hoop through his hands. "That's awesome!"

"Yes, with a little help from my mom and a YouTube video," Tobias said.

Declan's upbeat curiosity made Tobias wish he had told him sooner. He liked the feeling of sharing his sport with Declan. However, Tobias didn't want others at school to find out. Though he couldn't explain why.

"Please don't tell anyone at the school about my hoop dancing. Okay?" Tobias asked.

"Sure, I won't say anything, but can you teach me how you did the twirl spin move?" Declan's eyes grew large. They always did when he learned something new.

Tobias spent the next fifteen minutes teaching Declan how to hold the hoop and do three simple moves. He showed his friend a hand twirl, a finger twirl, and how to use two hoops to imitate a turtle snap.

Declan was a lot better than Tobias thought he would be. Before Tobias knew it, they were tossing a hoop back and forth, doing turn butt-kicks before tossing. Even though hoop dancing was a solo sport, Tobias enjoyed dancing alongside his friend.

"So. Why didn't you tell me about your hoop dancing?" Declan asked. He tossed a hoop to Tobias.

Tobias caught the hoop and paused. He had to be honest.

Finally, he said, "Sometimes you can be a loudmouth and tell people things without realizing it's not your place to tell them."

"You're not wrong. It's my worst flaw," Declan said. "But why don't you want anyone else to know?"

Again Tobias paused. What he was about to tell Declan was personal.

"I'm not very good," he finally said. "Plus, most people in our town have never heard of hoop dancing."

"I think you're good. And who cares if no one around here has heard of it," Declan said. "Toss the hoop back."

Tobias tossed it back, doing a one-armed cartwheel.

"See? What you just did, that was cool," Declan said. "Is this why you dance? So you can do all the cool tricks?"

Tobias shrugged. He couldn't explain his reasons; he was still figuring them out. Was it just cool tricks or was it deeper than that?

Tobias just hoped he could trust Declan with his secret.

CHAPTER 3

WHEN HOOPS FALL

Several weeks had passed since Tobias told Declan about his hoop dancing. Most mornings Declan would come over and help with the equipment and music.

This morning Tobias was alone working on a routine he was putting together. Declan had homework he needed to finish before school.

Sweat poured down Tobias's back, despite the cooler weather. His legs ached, and he was breathing hard. He yanked the hoop over his head for the fourth time, and it slapped him in the back.

"Ugh!"

Hoop jumps were like jumping rope. But instead of ropes, dancers used hoops, squatting as they jumped. Tobias hadn't gotten more than three hoop jumps in a row before he fell, fumbled, or slapped himself.

Tobias threw the hoop. It rolled a foot before it tumbled over.

To shake off his anger and frustration, Tobias grabbed three hoops and worked through a series of hoop moves. The movements always gave him peace.

He closed his eyes and listened to the steady beat of the drums. Starting with three hoops interlocked across his back, he popped up two more hoops, one in each hand.

His hoop moves were clunky. The magic of the dance came in the illusion of the hoop movement. His steps weren't perfect, but they were even.

He spanned the hoops across his back and arms but dropped one when his hand cramped.

When he was done, he noticed his mom watching him from the back porch.

"Looking good, Tobias. Your time practicing is starting to show." Mom smiled and stepped toward him.

Tobias smiled back. He felt the compliment down to his toes. He couldn't remember the last time his mom had watched him practice or encouraged his dancing.

She put her arm around him. "If you want, I can help you work on your balance and footing," she offered. "That should help with the hoop jumping. Fancy footwork takes a lot of practice."

"I would like that. Maybe tonight?" Tobias asked with hope in his voice.

Mom patted him on the head, pulling off his bandana. "Time for breakfast. Come inside before your eggs get cold."

His sisters, Mary and Anne, were already at the kitchen table eating cereal. They were eleven and five years old. Mom beelined to the counter and poured herself a cup of coffee. Tobias sat between his sisters and dug into his eggs.

Anne sang at the top of her lungs while crunching her cereal, "Twinkle, twinkle little star . . ."

"Anne!" Mom said. "Can you sing quietly?"

"Mom? Mom?" Mary repeated, trying to get Mom's attention. "I need new piano sheet music. Anne and I are doing a duet for the annual Spring Show. She'll sing of course."

Mom didn't answer. She was scrolling on her phone.

"Mom!" Mary yelled, spraying milk out her mouth. "Can you take me to the store after school? Sheet music is on sale this week."

"I'm sorry. There is a big project at work due today. I'll be at the office late getting it wrapped up. Maybe this weekend," Mom responded.

She looked at Tobias. "Can you take care of dinner tonight? I'll leave money on the table for a pizza."

"Sure, Mom." Tobias's head dropped.

It looked like he wouldn't get a practice session with his mom after all. He wished his mom had more time for them. Lately, she was always working. He didn't mind taking care of his little sisters, but it was a lot of responsibility. And he missed his mom too.

CHAPTER 4

NO ROBOTS HERE

After breakfast, Tobias grabbed his backpack from the couch in the living room and headed out the door. His sisters were already waiting outside for him under the big oak tree in their front lawn. Declan was waiting too.

"Sorry I missed your practice this morning. How'd it go?" Declan asked.

Tobias hitched his backpack higher on his shoulder. "Alright. I still can't get the hoop jump."

"He can't jump!" Mary and Anne yelled together and ran ahead of the boys.

Tobias ran his hand through his hair. Their words stung.

"Don't let the girls get to you," Declan added. "You'll get there."

"Oh, really?" Tobias rolled his eyes. "How do you know?" He sounded sarcastic, but Tobias really wanted to know the answer.

Declan stopped and looked at Tobias. "I think you just need to relax. You try too hard," he said.

Tobias rolled his eyes again. Somehow, Declan had become his unofficial coach.

Once they arrived at school, a single-story building that housed all grades from kindergarten to twelfth grade, the girls headed toward their side of the building.

Tobias looked at his watch. They had ten minutes before class, so they stopped at the open area near the entrance of the secondary school. A few kids were hanging around, but otherwise they were alone.

"Hey, I watched this video from this master hoop dancer," Declan said. "At least, that's what the video said. Anyway, he did this neat trick."

"Is this why you had to do homework this morning?" Tobias asked.

"Maybe. But anyway, he did this kick out leg thing, while twirling and twisting two hoops, one on each side."

Declan demonstrated. He stuck out an arm and a leg and pretended to twirl and hopped around. Declan's coordination wasn't on beat, but it wasn't bad.

Tobias lifted his arm and repeated the move himself. He just needed to find the beat first before diving in full force.

"Declan!" came a voice.

Their classmate Josh walked up. Tobias hadn't noticed Josh nearby.

"You look like a jittery robot," Josh teased.

Joel, Josh's best friend, laughed and pointed. "You too, Tobias," he said.

A group formed around the four boys.

Tobias's eyes flashed with anger. "That's not what it looks like."

Josh and Joel were in the same grade as Tobias and Declan, but they weren't friends. Ever since the spitball war in first grade, Tobias and Declan kept their distance from them. Over the years, Josh and Joel's snide remarks had grown stronger and more hurtful.

"Then what is it?" Joel asked. He stepped closer to Tobias.

"Yeah, what is it?" Josh repeated.

Declan answered, "I'm hoop dancing. It's a Native American dance, done at powwows."

Tobias held his breath. He hoped Declan would stop there.

"Ask Tobias, he's a hoop dancer," Declan proudly added, puffing his chest out.

The air left Tobias's lungs. Not only did Josh and Joel mock hoop dancing, but now they knew his secret. They would never leave him alone after this.

"Ha-ha, Tobias is a robot dancer." Joel mimicked the dance, jerking his body around. He did look like a robot.

Tobias's anger grew. His hands were balled at his sides. "Cut it out, Joel."

"I'm sorry, Tobias. It just came out," Declan said. He hung his head low.

The first bell rang, and Tobias stomped to first period. He needed space from Josh, Joel, and Declan to sort his thoughts.

CHAPTER 5

KEEPING COOL

Sweat dotted Tobias's brow. He was thick into his morning dance routine, doing double time to build endurance. His hands and legs were moving to the beat and the hoops were flying.

It had been almost a week since Declan spilled Tobias's secret. He wasn't so angry at Declan anymore. In a way, Tobias was relieved to have the secret out. However, he wasn't ready to admit that to Declan. Nor was he ready to ask him to come back to morning practice.

Twirl. Twist. Kick back.

The grass beneath his bare feet helped him feel grounded. To the earth, to the dance. He pushed everything else to the side.

Twirl. Twist. Kick back. Spin.

Tobias felt the energy move through him. The beat of the drum became him.

But the word *robot* came back to him. Josh and Joel's teasing had only intensified. Fear pulled in his stomach. Since that day, every morning and afternoon Josh and Joel made a joke of hoop dancing. Those boys didn't understand hoop dancing or its history. Their words and actions cut Tobias deeply.

Plus, everyone at school kept asking Tobias about hoop dancing. Tobias felt like he was in the spotlight, and he wasn't sure he liked it.

It was kind of like the time when Declan's mom made him do a year of Irish step dance. No one left Declan alone.

The sun rose higher. Tobias had about fifteen minutes left before he needed to go inside. He pushed thoughts of Josh and Joel down and picked up three additional hoops. By the end of school year, he hoped to dance with five hoops.

It wasn't easy. He wore three interlocking hoops across his shoulders like a jacket and popped two additional hoops into his hand with his right foot. The pop up was messy and super choppy.

He repeated the pop up move several times. On the last time, he moved one hoop to each hand. Tobias created a span from finger to finger. Like that of an eagle's wingspan.

He felt free. He soared. The wind moved through his hair as he twirled. He was flying.

The music came to a halt.

His moment of freedom was gone. Tobias opened his eyes.

"Time for breakfast, Tobias." Mom stood smiling. "It's your favorite—fry bread with powdered sugar."

Mom rarely made fry bread. Tobias's stomach grumbled.

"Mom, do you think you would have time tonight to give me some pointers?" His mom still hadn't made time to help him. "I know you didn't hoop dance, but you've been to a lot of powwows." Tobias removed the hoops and packed them in his bag.

Mom put her arm around Tobias, taking his bag from him. "Maybe this weekend. Work has piled up again."

Tobias pulled out of her arms. When would she make time for him?

"Are you okay? You seem upset. Is something bothering you?" Mom asked as she held the back door open.

"I'm fine, Mom," Tobias said. He stomped past the breakfast of sweet fry bread and headed for the shower.

Not only was he upset with Josh and Joel, but now with his mom too. It seemed like no one understood him. He helped Mom and his sisters all the time, but she never had time for him anymore.

Tobias's wet hair clung to his forehead as walked to the front door. His sisters were waiting for him.

"I'll leave money for pizza," Mom called from the kitchen. "Please keep an eye on your sisters."

Tobias slammed the door as he left the house.

CHAPTER 6

THE ANNOUNCEMENT

Tobias ran down the steps of the porch and pushed past his sisters and Declan. He felt guilty for slamming the door but not guilty enough to go back and apologize to his mom.

"Hey, wait up!" Declan jogged up, out of breath. "Are you okay?"

"I'm fine. Just stuff at home," Tobias answered, kicking a rock on the sidewalk.

"Tobias is being a poopy-head." Anne laughed, joining the pair.

"Don't call him a poopy-head. He's more like a big jerk," Mary grumbled. She said it under her breath, but it was loud enough for Tobias and Declan to hear.

Tobias kept quiet, but his anger kept building.

Anne stepped in front of Tobias and with her hands on her hips yelled, "POOPY-HEAD!" Then she ran away, giggling.

"Your little sister isn't wrong. In this case, the name fits," Declan pointed out.

Tobias sighed. He guessed he *was* being a poopy-head to his sisters and Declan. His mom too. But sometimes it was really hard to stop being angry.

"Oh, forgot to mention. I came across Cody Sherman. The hoop dancer from Oklahoma. Have you heard of him?" Declan asked.

The mention of Cody Sherman chiseled away a bit of Tobias's anger.

"Cody is one of the best hoop dancers of all time. Watching him dance is how I learned to interlock hoops. His tutorial videos are golden," Tobias said.

"I watched most of his videos last night," Declan said. "He's a good instructor. I even tried to do some of his steps."

Declan stopped and bounced up and down on his feet, tapping twice on each foot.

"Oh, yeah. Can you do this one?" Tobias did a side-step bounce trot.

Mary and Anne raced back and joined in the dance. The girls spun as they bounced, moving their arms up and down as if they had hoops.

Tobias smiled. A rush of adrenaline chased away his anger.

Declan stopped dancing and placed his hands on his knees to catch his breath.

P

"Are you still upset with me about telling Josh and Joel about your hoop dancing?" Declan asked.

"I don't think so," Tobias finally said. "In one of his videos, Cody said that dancing is a form of community. I had forgotten about that."

They arrived at school and, for the first time in weeks, walked in together as a group.

A small crowd huddled around the main announcement board in the foyer. As they moved closer, they read SPRING TALENT SHOW in big block letters.

The show was two weeks away, but auditions were in three days. The auditions were not competitive. Pretty much everyone who auditioned made it into the show.

Tobias's sisters squealed. Mary hummed a tune while Anne sang their duet piece. This was the first year they could perform together.

Tobias had been so distracted with hoop dancing (and being mad at his mom) that he had forgotten about the annual talent show. He looked forward to watching his sisters perform.

Tobias and Declan were the last to arrive to class. Josh and Joel were already in their seats and looked ready to pounce.

"Hey, Tobias. You gonna hoop dance for everyone at the talent show?" Josh asked loudly. "Maybe you and Declan can do a duo like your sisters."

"Yeah, we want to see you do your robot dance," Joel added, with a clunky shoulder roll dance move.

The normally loud room grew quiet. Everyone looked at Tobias, waiting for his answer.

Tobias had had enough. He decided he would fight back by dancing at the talent show.

"Whatever I do will be better than what you two got," he said.

"What Josh and I perform at the talent show will blow away your dance. Can't wait to see you fail," Joel growled.

CHAPTER 7

AUDITIONS

The cool mornings from the week before had turned humid the day of tryouts for the Spring Talent Show. Sticky sweat poured down Tobias's back.

He was anxious for the audition, even though everyone who auditioned made it into the show. He was worried he would make a mistake. And what would others think of his dancing? This would be his first time dancing in front of a crowd.

Tobias pushed those thoughts aside. He had just enough time to go through his two-minute routine once more before breakfast. He placed the hoops on the ground and nodded to Declan to start the music.

"You got this, Tobias," Declan said.

Using both feet, Tobias popped the hoops into his hands. One in his left, the other in his right. He started with traditional footwork while spinning and twirling the hoops.

From there, keeping the same beat, he repeated the move. But this time he turned clockwise in a continuous circle, moving the hoops faster. Next, he faced Declan and changed his footwork, moving his left leg to the back and then to the front. Then he switched legs.

For his finale, Tobias popped another hoop into his hand. He quickly interlocked all three across his back, like he was wearing a jacket.

He then popped two more hoops up, one in each hand. Five hoops spanned across his back and to his arms. Like an eagle flying, he spun in a circle as he danced.

As the last beat ended, Tobias grinned.

"*AIEEEE!* I did it! Declan, I did it!" Tobias shouted, unlocking the hoops. "*AIEEEE!*"

Declan jumped up and gave him a high five. "You did it!"

* * *

The school day dragged on, and Tobias was jittery all day. By the time everyone gathered in the auditorium for tryouts, Tobias was ready to turn on his music and dance.

On stage, the talent show director gave a few directions to organize the students. "Group and solo acts, please pick up a number. Groups one through ten, line up in order. Everyone else, stay seated and line up when called."

Tobias and his sisters were numbered six and seven. Josh and Joel's duo were five.

"Don't give them any thought," Declan said. He nodded toward the duo.

Josh and Joel had on white gym shorts and bright blue jerseys. Joel held a bright pink football. They ignored Tobias. But as their number was called, Josh turned toward him.

"Get ready," he said. "You're about to watch the best."

Pop music blared from the overhead speakers. Josh and Joel did a football dance routine, starting with a huddle to a kickoff to a pass to a touchdown.

Throughout, they added in twirls and leaps keeping in time with the music. They ended with a synchronized cheerleader straight jump, followed by a hurdler, and finished with toe touch.

Everyone applauded, including Mary and Anne. While Josh and Joel weren't perfect, they did entertain the crowd.

"Beat that," Joel spat out.

Tobias tightened his bandana and walked on stage.

Declan shot him a thumbs-up.

The drumbeat synced with Tobias's heartbeat. He worked through his routine flawlessly. Near the end, though, as he placed his foot on the last two hoops to make his span of five, his foot slipped. And he fell. The hoops bounced and rolled away.

Josh and Joel laughed.

Tobias, embarrassed and ashamed, stormed off the stage.

CHAPTER 8

TIME OFF

Tobias grabbed his hoops and sat in the back of the auditorium. He was fuming and didn't want to talk to anyone. Not even Declan. Josh and Joel were right, they were better than him. His legs bounced up and down as his sisters went through their duet.

Once his sisters were done, he whisked them home. Declan tried to talk to him, but Tobias only grunted short responses.

That night, as he lay in bed, he heard his mom open his door. "Tobias, do you want to talk about today?" she asked.

With his back to the door, Tobias pretended to be asleep. He was still mad at his mom for not helping him. Maybe if she had given him some advice and direction, he wouldn't have failed in front of the entire school.

Over the next several days, Tobias slept in. He ignored his alarm clock and the hoops. With five days until the talent show, Tobias decided he was dropping out of the show. Declan tried to talk him out of it, but Tobias wouldn't budge.

Two days later his mom confronted him in his room. "Tobias, you haven't been practicing the past few mornings. Do you want to talk about it? Mary told me you are planning to drop out of the talent show."

"Nope, don't want to talk," Tobias answered, working on a math assignment.

He knew his mom would eventually expect him to talk, but he wasn't going to make it easy for her.

His mom sat down on his bed. "I am sorry I haven't been there for you lately. I've put a lot of pressure on you. Work has been busy, but the responsibility of your sisters shouldn't have fallen on you."

"Mom, I don't mind watching Mary and Anne," Tobias replied.

"Then what is it? It's not like you to give up on something," his mom said.

Tobias thought about his response. "I don't think I can dance anymore. Once everyone found out about my hoop dancing, some kids made fun of the dance. Most people don't even know what hoop dancing is. Then I messed up my routine at the tryouts."

His mom listened.

"Maybe hoop dancing isn't for me," Tobias continued. "Besides videos, and that one powwow, I haven't had any one-on-one instruction. It's hard when it feels like you're on your own."

"You're right, and I'm sorry about that. When I gave up ballet, that was the hardest decision of my life," his mom said. "But hoop dancing is different with you. That kind of dancing comes from your heart, and that's where the beauty lies. It's not about perfection. It's about connection to the stories around us."

His mom gave him a hug. "Take the time you need to decide," she added.

After Tobias finished his homework, he lay in bed. He was just about to drift off when his phone pinged.

Declan: Check out this new video from Cody Sherman

Tobias's finger hovered over the link. He clicked it.

The video was simple. Cody Sherman danced to a song. No instruction or voice over was given. The only description came from the title, "Me and My Hoops."

As he watched the dancer, Tobias's fingers itched to hold a hoop, and his feet moved to the beat, wanting to touch the ground and dance.

Tobias knew that hoop dancing told a story, one that remembered the past and looked toward the future. But what he realized in that moment was that it also told his story.

CHAPTER 9

HOOPING AGAIN

The next morning, Tobias woke to his alarm. The sun had just risen over the horizon. He had time to think about Cody Sherman's video. Before he got up, he took a deep breath.

His phone pinged.

Declan: Practice this morning?

Tobias: Meet you out back in five

Tobias dressed, throwing on basketball shorts, a sweatshirt, and shoes. He ran his hand through his hair and tied a red bandana around his head. He grabbed his equipment bag from his closet.

The morning air cleared his thoughts.

"I knew the video would work," Declan said when he saw Tobias. They walked together shoulder to shoulder. "I thought we could record using your phone so we can work through any issues. I'll get the music ready."

Tobias handed over his phone.

"No words this morning?" asked Declan. "Okay. I'll take that to mean you're focusing your energy on your routine."

"Sorry, Declan. I'm just not ready to talk. Maybe the dancing will help," Tobias responded.

He was frustrated with himself. He needed to heal with the hoops.

Silently, the boys laid out the hoops.

Tobias walked over to his starting position as Declan got the phone ready to record.

Tobias warmed up his body, first by jumping and then jogging in place. He shook out his arms, hands, legs, and feet. Blood pumped through his body. After ten minutes of stretching deep and long, the way his mom had taught him when he first started dancing, he was ready.

Declan broke the silence. “Ready when you are,” he said.

Tobias nodded.

The music was low but loud enough for Tobias to feel each beat. He began slowly, letting his feet find the rhythm. Each time his foot met the ground, he felt more connected to the song and to each movement. His feet moved faster. His hands too.

As Tobias neared the end of the routine, his mind eased. His five hoop wings spread easily. His dance had been perfect.

"Tobias, that was great!" Declan ran up to him, the playback already playing on the phone. "You were in the zone."

For the next fifteen minutes, he and Declan analyzed each step, turn, and twirl.

Breakfast was a combination of oatmeal, eggs, and toast. His sisters had already eaten and were in the living room practicing their duet.

"Glad to see you were out with Declan this morning." Mom poured herself a cup of coffee. "Does this mean you're back to hoop dancing?"

"Mmmph," Tobias grunted. He wasn't ready to agree with his mom by giving a direct answer.

* * *

Later, when the lunch bell rang, Tobias and Declan headed toward the cafeteria.

"I just hope they aren't serving spaghetti, because every time I always get a side of hair. Try pulling that out of your teeth," Declan said. "Yuck."

Tobias laughed.

"Finally!" Declan cried as they joined the back of the lunch line. "I knew I could get you to laugh. So. Spring Talent Show? You in?"

Before Tobias could respond, Josh and Joel got in line behind them.

"Heard you dropped out of the talent show. Figures," Josh said.

"He'd probably just drop his hoops again," Joel added. "Hey, I guess that could be a talent: Clumsy Tobias and the Tumbling Tower of Hoops."

Tobias stood tall but didn't respond. He knew what he needed to do.

CHAPTER 10

THE SPRING SHOW OFF

The morning of the Spring Talent Show, every light in Tobias's house was on when his alarm sounded. Mary and Anne were already practicing their duet, and he could hear their mom in the kitchen.

Tobias stepped into the kitchen and found Declan rolling out biscuit dough.

"You're finally up," Declan said as he wiped flour off his hands. "I came over early to make sure you were up."

"Good morning, Tobias," Mom said. "Want anything special for breakfast this morning? The girls asked for biscuits and gravy."

"Nothing special for me. Thanks, Mom," Tobias answered. He turned to Declan and asked, "You ready?"

The boys set up the area and went through the routine three times. On the last round, just as Tobias finished his eagle spin, he saw his mom watching from the back porch.

"Tobias." Mom came over to give him a big bear hug. "I didn't realize you could dance like that. I should have paid more attention to you. I'm sorry. So sorry." Mom wiped tears from her eyes. "Your dancing was beautiful."

Tobias leaned into her hug. "Thank you, Mom."

"Whoa. There is a lot of emotion here," Declan said. "Tobias, I'll meet you and your sisters out front after breakfast."

Tobias laughed. He felt good for the first time in a long time.

Mom helped Tobias pick up his hoops. "I know I've missed so much, with you and your sisters. Things will change. I've already made arrangements at work. I'll be home more."

"Does this mean you can give me some more dance tips? Declan and I have lots of video that could use your expert eye," Tobias said.

"I'd be honored to help," Mom said. "Maybe I can start with laying out your regalia. Not that there is anything wrong with dancing in shorts. But tonight is special."

Tobias smiled. "I'd like that." He hadn't worn his Choctaw regalia—black shorts, a Choctaw diamond shirt and apron, and a beaded medallion and sweatband—since the last powwow. He could feel the strength of his ancestors. They would be with him as he danced.

* * *

The lights flickered in the auditorium. The Spring Talent Show was about to begin. Tobias, his sisters, and Declan were seated near the front in the performers' section.

Josh and Joel opened the show. Again, they brought down the house. Mary and Anne were next and were adorable. They got a standing ovation even when Anne sang off-key.

Tobias's dance was the last performance of the evening. The audience had grown restless after two hours of talent. Declan walked backstage with him.

"You got this, Tobias. Your fancy regalia will hook them, but only you can deliver. Give them what you did this morning," Declan said. "You're going to be great."

"Declan, I couldn't have done this without you. Thanks for everything," Tobias said. "I'm sorry I kept my dancing a secret from you."

"We all have our secrets. I mean, I only told you about my Irish step dancing because my mom told your mom," Declan replied.

Tobias was announced. The music started, and he stepped out on stage.

All the anger he held inside slipped away. Piece by piece, it vanished until all that was left was him and his hoops. His reasons for dancing had nothing to do with being perfect and everything to do with connections. His family and his ancestors. His friends and his community.

And most of all he realized, hoop dancing healed his heart.

AUTHOR BIO

Stacy Wells loves playing sports, especially soccer. However, she has two left feet when it comes to dancing. Her lack of dancing skills didn't stop her from devouring all things hoop dancing. Stacy is a member of the Choctaw Nation and lives in Texas with her family, including a red dog named Blu and a ferret that goes by Stan.

ILLUSTRATOR BIO

Jesus Aburto has worked in the comic book industry for more than eleven years. In that time, he has illustrated popular characters such as Wolverine, Iron Man, Blade, and the Punisher. Recently, Jesus started his own illustration studio called Graphikslava. He lives in Monterrey, Mexico, with his kids Ilka, Mila, Aleph, and his beloved wife.

GLOSSARY

ancestors (AN-ses-turs)—family members who lived a long time ago

Choctaw Nation (CHOK-taw NAY-shuhn)—a Native sovereign nation in southeast Oklahoma

coordination (koh-OR-duh-nay-shuhn)—the ability to control body movements

endurance (en-DUR-enss)—the ability to keep doing an activity for long periods of time

flexibility (flek-suh-BIL-i-tee)—the ability to bend or move easily

fry bread (FRYE-bred)—a flat bread made from fried dough that is a signature food among many Native communities

illusion (i-LOO-zhuhn)—something that appears to be real but isn't

interlock (in-ter-LOCK)—to interweave or interlace, one with another

powwow (POW-wow)—a gathering of Native Americans featuring traditional dances and music

regalia (ri-GAY-lee-uh)—the special clothing a Native dancer wears during traditional dances

MORE ABOUT HOOP DANCING

The history of Indigenous hoop dancing is dynamic, with many different origin stories spanning across various Native nations. Today, it is a popular storytelling dance at powwows in the United States and Canada. Indigenous people from all nations and tribes can participate in this unique dance style.

Hoop dancing is an individual dance that can be performed by anyone, regardless of gender or age. The hoops are moved around the whole body, using hands, arms, legs, and feet.

Each dancer brings their own style, artistry, and cultural traditions to their dance. More advanced dancers can have up to 40 or more hoops going at one time. Just like in other sports, dancers need to practice often to grow their skills and keep them sharp.

Traditionally, hoops were made from willow branches. Now it's common to use plastic tubing. Colored electrical tape is used to decorate them. Some use the tape to mark the four directions: north, south, east, and west. However, there are many variations, depending on the dancer.

Every year, the Heard Museum in Arizona hosts the World Championship Hoop Dance event. Dancers are grouped according to their age and judged in five areas: precision, timing and rhythm, showmanship, creativity, and speed. Prize money is given in every age group, and one dancer from each age group is given the title World Champion.

If you can, try to attend a public powwow. The sights and sounds are an experience like no other.

DISCUSSION QUESTIONS

1. Tobias's family supported his hoop dancing. However, he also had a lot of responsibility at home, taking care of his sisters while his mom worked. How did this make Tobias feel?

2. Declan told a secret he wasn't supposed to tell. However, Declan made up for his mistake in several ways. List evidence from the text.

3. Why do you think Josh and Joel were so mean to Tobias?

WRITING PROMPTS

1. Tobias learned to hoop dance by watching others dance. How do you learn new things?

2. Write about a time you did something brave. How did it make you feel?

3. Pretend you're on stage showcasing a talent. What would it be? It can be something you're good at or hope to be good at someday. Why did you pick that talent?